The HARBOR LIGHT

Written and Illustrated by
Eric Walls

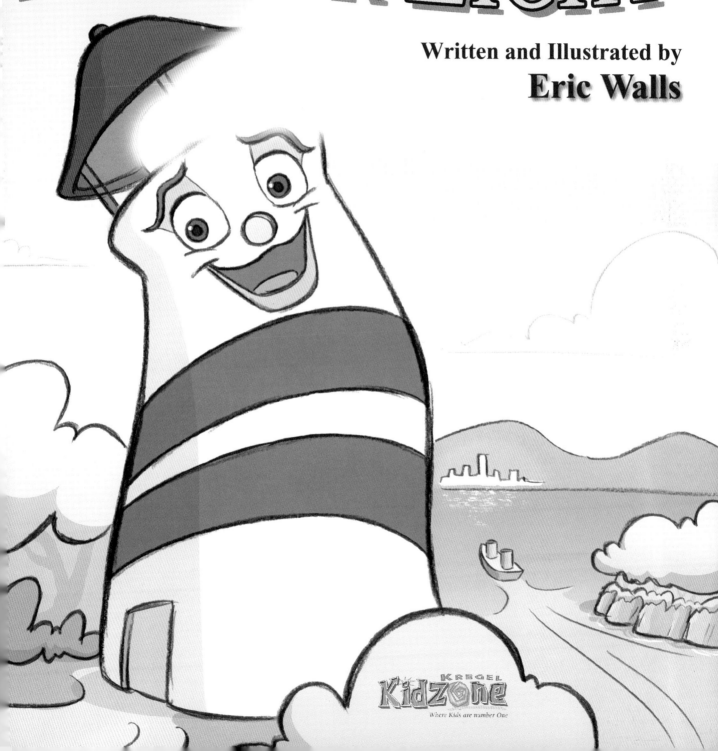

KREGEL Kidzone — Where Kids are number One

*In memory of
my father,
Rev. Robert Walls,
who lived his life
as a lighthouse.*

The Harbor Light
© 2005 by Eric Walls

Published by Kregel Kidzone, an imprint of Kregel Publications, P.O. Box 2607, Grand Rapids, MI 49501.

All Scripture quotations are taken from the Holy Bible, New International Version®. NIV®. Copyright © 1973, 1978, 1984 by International Bible Society. Used by permission of Zondervan. All rights reserved.

ISBN 0-8254-4155-2

Printed in China

High on a cliff by the ocean, at the entrance to a harbor, stood a little lighthouse.

He loved to spend the day looking at all the wonderful sights around him.

"Wow!" the lighthouse said. "I wish *I* could play all day too!"

But being a lighthouse, he always had to keep his light shining so that all the boats could find their way safely to the harbor.

"If only I didn't have to keep my light on," he thought, "then I could have fun too!"

After thinking it over, he said to himself, "What would it hurt if I turned it off for just a little while?" So when no one was looking . . .

He turned off his light.
"Oh, how wonderful!" he thought. "Now I can do what I want!"
But at that moment, he heard a familiar voice.

"Lighthouse, what's wrong with your light?"
It was the friendly lighthouse keeper, who always made sure the lighthouse was working well.
"Oh, nothing," the lighthouse said, quickly turning his light back on.

"Lighthouse," the keeper said, "you must always keep your light on so the boats can find their way to the harbor."
"I'm sorry, sir," the lighthouse replied. "It won't happen again. You can count on me!"
After the keeper left, the lighthouse thought about what he had done.
But then suddenly he heard a noise.

A speedboat moved through the water with ease, jumping
over the waves and doing tricks in the air.
The lighthouse had never seen anything so exciting!

"Hello," the lighthouse called to the boat. "How do you do those amazing tricks?"

"They're easy," answered the boat in an angry voice. He did not like being bothered by the lighthouse.

"I thought we could be friends," the lighthouse said to the boat.

The boat laughed. "Friends? I could never be friends with somebody who always shines that silly light!"

"But the boats need it to find their way to the harbor," said the lighthouse.

"The harbor?" laughed the boat. "I don't need the harbor *or* your silly light! I can take care of myself."

The lighthouse was embarrassed, but he really wanted to be friends with the boat.

"Would you stay if I turned my light off?"

"Well," the boat said, "I might if you promise to keep it off."

"I promise!"

And after making sure no one else was looking,

. . . he turned off his light again.

Now the boat, being a little bit mean, had only pretended to be the lighthouse's friend. He thought it would be fun to get the lighthouse into trouble.

"How about *you* doing a trick?" the boat said.

"I don't think I can," the lighthouse said shyly.

"Do a trick or I'll leave," the boat insisted.

After the lighthouse thought for a moment about what trick he could do to impress the boat, he said, "Watch this."

The lighthouse leaped high into the air with all his might.
But when he landed . . .

The boat just laughed at the sight.

"What happened?" the lighthouse keeper called as he ran up to investigate the noise.

"Oh, nothing much," the lighthouse said, trying to appear calm.

"But you're broken!" the keeper said. "What were you doing?"

"Just a little trick," the lighthouse replied. "It's no big deal. My light still works."

After struggling a moment, he clicked his light back on.

"See?"

The keeper looked really worried. "Lighthouse, you weren't made for that type of activity," he said.

"Oh, it really isn't that bad," the lighthouse replied. "*Most* of me is in one piece!"

"But you must do your job with your *whole* self," the keeper said. "If part of you is broken, the rest of you won't work as well as it should."

With that, the keeper left. The lighthouse thought about what the keeper said, but he still wanted the boat to like him. So when the keeper was out of sight, he turned off his light once more.

"Oh boy!" the boat laughed. "He acts like you did something terrible."

"Yeah," the lighthouse said. "He always worries too much!"

"Hey," the boat replied. "Let's have some *real* fun now! Watch this."

The boat moved quickly toward a pair of dolphins.

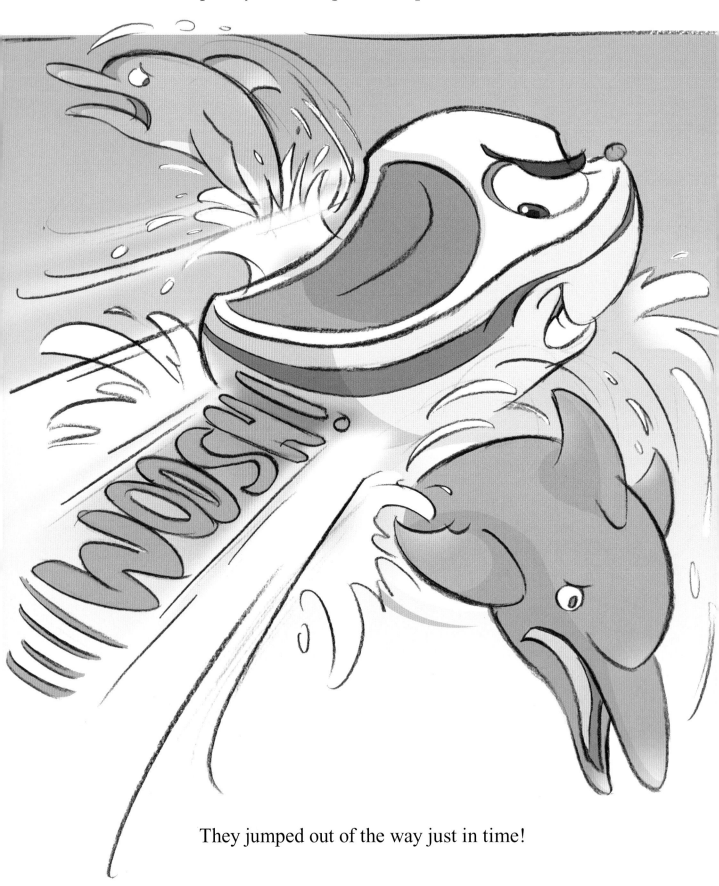

They jumped out of the way just in time!

The lighthouse laughed and laughed.

"That was funny!" the lighthouse said. "Now it's my turn!"

He looked around and saw a group of seagulls flying toward him.

"Watch this!" he whispered to the boat as he hid from the birds.

At first the lighthouse laughed, but then he saw what he had done.

"I'm sorry," he said to the seagulls. "I didn't mean to hurt anyone.
Please come back, I was just having a little fun."
But the seagulls were too frightened, and they flew away.

"You don't actually care about them, do you?" the boat asked.

"I just didn't mean to hurt them," replied the lighthouse sadly.

"Who cares?" said the boat, turning to leave. "I thought you were going to be cool, but you're no fun at all."

Soon the boat was out of sight, and the lighthouse was all alone and very sad.

After a few hours, dark storm clouds began to roll in and the waves grew big. The lighthouse knew that his light would be needed in such a terrible storm. But when he tried to turn it back on, it wouldn't work.

"Oh no," he said to himself. "I broke it. What am I going to do now?"

He knew that the little boat must be lost out in the stormy sea.

As the rain poured down, the lighthouse felt helpless.

"That boat needs your help," said a familiar voice.

It was the lighthouse keeper.
"Someone else will have to save him," said the lighthouse quietly. "My light is broken."

"It's still there, if you believe," said the keeper. "But you must never hide it again. Always keep it shining bright."

"That boat will be lost. Will you show him the way?"

"The keeper is right," he thought.
"It *is* my job to guide the boats to safety. But my light is broken."
Or was it?

He so very much wanted his light to shine again.
So, he concentrated with all his heart and all his might.
And suddenly . . .

Far away, the stormy waves
tossed the boat about. He was
so afraid.

But then he saw the light. He was saved!
And so, following the light, he found his way
to the harbor.

The boat was ashamed of how he had treated the lighthouse.

"I'm really sorry," the boat said. "Can you ever forgive me for being so mean?"

"Oh, yes," the lighthouse replied. "And I'm sorry too. I never should have done anything to harm my light.

"Now, come into the harbor," said the lighthouse. "You'll be safe there."

So the little boat happily entered the harbor.

"I'm sorry," said the lighthouse to the keeper. "I should have listened to you! Now I know why it's so important to keep my light working."

"And remember," said the keeper, "always let your light shine so that others may see it and follow it to safety."

"Oh, yes!" said the lighthouse. "I'll never hide my light again!" And he never did.

"Well done, lighthouse," said the keeper. "Well done."

NOTE TO PARENTS

Just like the little lighthouse in this story, we too are called to shine a light in our dark world. Jesus said, "You are the light of the world. A city on a hill cannot be hidden. Neither do people light a lamp and put it under a bowl. Instead they put it on its stand, and it gives light to everyone in the house. In the same way, let your light shine before men, that they may see your good deeds and praise your Father in heaven (Matthew 5:14-16 NIV). Not only should we live as a good example so that others will be encouraged to be better, but it is our duty as Christians to show the lost the good and wonderful things that God can do in a person's life. We are to be the means through which He draws the lost to Himself, to His safe harbor.

After reading the book, begin a discussion with your children about the story. Does it remind them of people they know or a situation they have been in? If your children have already accepted Christ, encourage them to live the love of God and be a light to their friends. If your children haven't yet found Him, use this story as a springboard to discuss salvation. Have they ever felt lonely and scared, like the little boat lost at sea, without a sense of direction? Wouldn't a light, brightly shining through the storm, give them relief and guidance? Jesus can be that light if we choose to follow Him.